To Mia

God has not given us
a spirit of fear, but of
power, love and a
sound mind.
2 Tim 1:7

God created a garden paradise so that man might freely meet
with Him there. Instead, man created a box called religion in-
which he tries to meet with God there. The sad thing is, that
from inside the empty box, he can not hear the voice of his
Creator calling him to break free and come back to the garden.

George Paul Youket

Blessings
George Youket
1/20/2018

God created man in His own image, in the image of God
He created him; male and female He created them.

Genesis 1:27

THE ADAM CHRONICLES

Adam and Eve the Book

GEORGE PAUL YOUKET

WESTBOW®
PRESS
A DIVISION OF THOMAS NELSON
& ZONDERVAN

WestBow Press books may be ordered through booksellers or by contacting:

WestBow Press
A Division of Thomas Nelson & Zondervan
1663 Liberty Drive
Bloomington, IN 47403
www.westbowpress.com
1 (866) 928-1240

ISBN: 978-1-4908-5949-1 (sc)
ISBN: 978-1-4908-5951-4 (hc)
ISBN: 978-1-4908-5950-7 (e)

Library of Congress Control Number: 2014919974

Printed in the United States of America.

WestBow Press rev. date: 12/11/2014

Contents

Dedication vii

Foreword...ix

Preface xi

Acknowledgments xvii

Chapter 1   The Embrace..1

Chapter 2   The Garden..9

Chapter 3   The Tree 16

Chapter 4   The Woman...26

Chapter 5   The Dark Force Emerges...........................38

Chapter 6   The Temptation 43

Chapter 7   The Accusers...55

Chapter 8   Mans First Religion 62

Chapter 9   The Curse...69

Chapter 10 Redemption Revealed 73

Chapter 11 Life Outside the Garden 78

Chapter 12 The Anointed Seed is Preserved................86

End Notes...97

Dedication

I dedicate this book to Theresa, my beautiful and faithful
wife for the last thirty-six years, who gave me six wonderful
children… and apple pie!

He who finds a good wife finds a good thing
and obtains favor from the Lord.
Proverbs 18:22 (MIT)

Foreword

The Adam Chronicles sets us on an amazing journey. It's like stepping into a time machine that brings us back to our Paradise lost. It is where the imagination of our heart is purified through the source of unrestricted love. It will inspire you to think beyond your present beliefs that may have encased, limited, or hindered your understanding of Divine Love. The book dares us to experience the unlimited goodness of God by unveiling and illuminating the pathway that leads us back to our true home in Eden.

From the first chapter to the last, George brings a realistic sense of what it was like to be there. God suddenly becomes reachable, touchable, and real. The Christian god of mans creation, the god of anger, the old man in the sky, and the stoic religious figure, is replaced by the true Christian God of everlasting love, kindness and compassion. Coming to know and understand this makes us want to run into the arms of the God of the Garden. This God, by his own declaration is the same yesterday, today and forever.

Anyone who is seeking to understand the true heart of God, can find it in *The Adam Chronicles*. This book will bring to those of open mind a greater understanding and appreciation of God's love, manifested in and through the Author and Finisher of the Christian faith, Jesus Christ. It is He who opens hearts to purify imagination and so reveal truth by the Spirit of Grace.

May Grace abound to all those who read this book, and especially the Book of Books, the Bible. For the volume of that Book testifies of Him, the only true and living God who rose from the dead and now lives to make intercession for all men.

John Stolwyk
Director of: Eminent Grace for Daily Living

Preface

Who hasn't read the biblical account of creation without entertaining thoughts and speculations about what might have taken place between the lines of the actual events recorded? I am sure there are many who miss the truths revealed by the beautiful symbols and metaphors contained in the first three chapters of Genesis. Those who have never read the story, or have only a basic understanding of it, will especially appreciate this book. Beneath the surface of those chapters are truths and promises so beyond the imaginations and hopes of the average person, that even after seeing them are hard to believe.

Over the centuries, much of religion has grossly misrepresented God, portraying him as an angry deity just waiting for an opportunity to strike us with some horrible judgment or devastating plague. I want to dispel the idea that the God of the Bible is an angry, condemning, and vengeful God. His vengeance and wrath are actually directed toward anything that opposes his original purpose and plan for man, not man himself.[1] I believe that although God is just, he is by nature loving, and not only is it his nature, he is defined by love itself.[2]

From the beginning, God has desired to express his love for us, and to be joined with us in one inseparable union. To understand this is to comprehend the theme of the Bible and to begin to understand who our heavenly Father really is.[3]

God has always had only plans of good and not evil for mankind. His intentions have never been to bring harm to us, but to give us a hope and a future, a life of abundance.[4]

If you are like me, having always had a real fascination with the story of Adam and Eve, you will find this short novel thought provoking and reassuring of God's love. It will shine light upon many of the wonderful truths that might be missed by the casual reader of the Bible.

It will also, answer some of those puzzling questions that many of us entertain: Why was the Tree of the Knowledge of Good and Evil placed in the garden? No question or answer is more central to understanding our potential to accomplish or to destroy than the questions and answers regarding the primordial Tree of Knowledge of Good and Evil. It is one of the mysteries of mysteries revealed.

Other questions abound. Who has not wondered why Satan was allowed in the garden? What made Adam and

Eve suddenly aware of their nakedness? Where did Cain get his wife?" And so on.

Hopefully, you will also come to understand how much of the New Testament revelation is contained in the story of creation. I try to help connect the dots between the new and old covenants by showing the continuity between them. The truths of the New Testament are deeply hidden within the Old Testament pages and then revealed and explained in the New. The types and symbols in the Old Testament are shadows of what was to be revealed in and explained in the New Testament. Understanding these symbols and their significance gives the reader a renewed appreciation of the Bible.

Although I hold to the literal purpose and theme of the Scripture in this writing, I have added imagined events and dialog between the actual events that took place. I personally believe that the Bible's account of creation is true and factual, but it is not necessary to agree with that premise in order to appreciate the value of the story's importance in setting the tone and theme for the entire Bible.

Another of my objectives is to shine light upon the triune nature of God. He is one God, yet expressed through three distinct persons. Love necessitates this. God exists in three persons because love requires relationship, and without the relationship of Father, Son, and Holy Spirit, God could not be a God of love.[5] This is why Adam, who was made in God's image, was incomplete before Eve was taken out of him and given back to him in the form of a woman. A counterpart of himself had to be created, a being toward which he could express love. The mystery of the triune God is revealed and expressed through the union and relationship of man, wife, and offspring, through marriage and family.

My inspiration for this work came not only from forty years of study and Scripture translation, but primarily because of the great love of Him who loved me and saved me by His amazing grace: my Lord Jesus Christ. I will forever love Him and thank Him for the life eternal that He has given to me, and to all who will believe and call upon His name.

We are all on a journey in this life, searching for the answers to those great metaphysical questions: "Where did I come from?" "Why am I here?" And, "Where am I going after death?" It is my prayer that this book will play a part in helping many find the answers to those kinds of questions.

Every man and every woman was created with dignity and value. This was established within the heart of a loving God before He laid the foundations of this world. He desires that all people would come to know and understand not only their true value, but their origin, purpose, and destiny in life. These can be found only in a living relationship with Him.

Do not confuse my opinions as dogma. The content of this writing is not meant to be dogmatic, but rather to inspire thoughtful considerations of some truths revealed in the Bible's story of creation. I do not want to tell others what to think, but to encourage them just to think for themselves. We all need to constantly challenge our belief systems with opposing views to see if what we believe is actually supported by the girders of truth.

Acknowledgments

I would like to acknowledge some of the friends who helped me or inspired me in the writing of this work.

Barbara Paratore
Edward Youket
Frank W. Richardson
Jeff Creery
Jessie Monk
Kyle Burdick
MaryAnn Callahan
Teddy Stolwyk

Special thanks to my good friend and brother in Christ, John Stolwyk. John's scriptural advice and additions were invaluable.

Also, special thanks to Mark Winheld, a talented writer and published author of two great books. His recommendations and editing were so appreciated.

Also, to the teacher and mentor who first brought to me the knowledge of my true identity in Christ:

Bishop Malcolm Smith

The beautiful painting on the cover of this book was done by: Italia Ruotolo of Italy.

Chapter 1

The Embrace

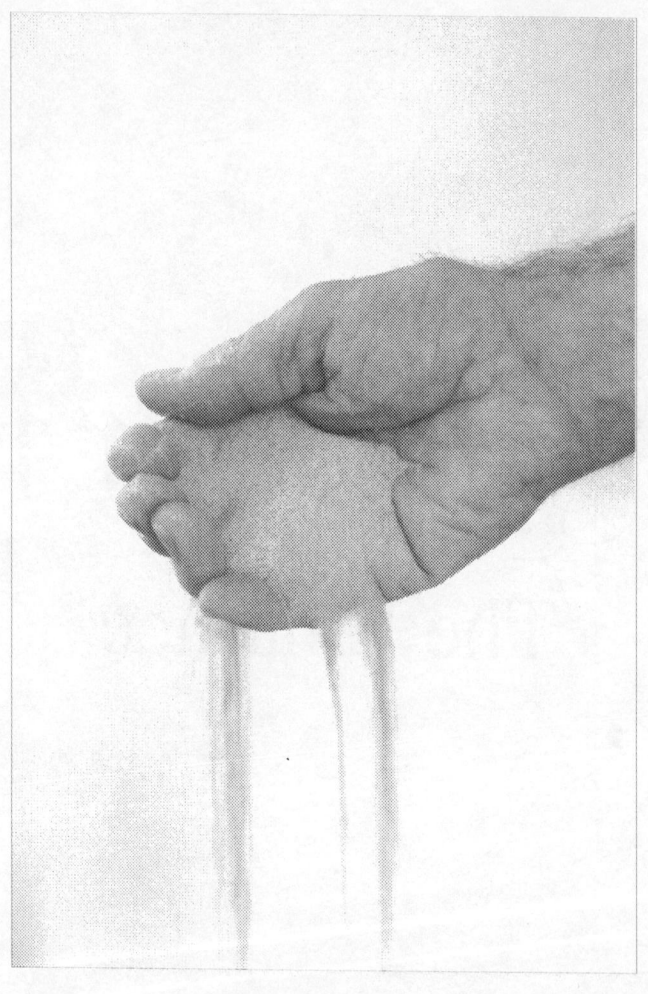

Then the LORD God formed man of dust from the
ground, and breathed into his nostrils the breath of life;
and man became a living being.

—Genesis 2:7

It was the first morning in the garden,[6] and the forest creatures awakened to the appearance of something strangely different and beautiful. There, lying in the cool of the morning, was a creature so unlike them. What kind of creature was this? Or was it a creature at all? No species like this had yet appeared in the garden.

As all the angels in Ooranos[7] (the heavenly realm) were watching, wide-eyed with amazement and great anticipation, the Creator took a deep breath and breathed into the nostrils of the still body. Suddenly, the creature began to move, unfolding his arms and legs from the fetal position in which he had been lying. His eyes opened and stared upward, slowly scanning back and forth trying to take in and comprehend all that was flooding his mind and soul. Sounds filled his ears, and rays of sunlight created feelings of warmth upon his body.

As he lay there gazing upward, another Being stood over him, a Being of indescribable beauty. Golden hair graced His head and shoulders, hair that seemed to be made of liquid crystal, like light itself. His eyes were like blue sapphires and were full of kindness. A smile creased his face with the countenance of grace, which gave the creature an immediate sense of peace.

A wonderful, indescribable force of well-being radiated from the Beings presence.

Suddenly the Being reached out and said, "Come, Adam (meaning man), rise up." Adam reached out instinctively and found the touch of the Being's hand was gentle and reassuring.

Adam thought to himself, *Where am I? And who is this?*

As Adam rose to his feet, he said to the Being, "Who are you, my Lord, and how is it that I am here and able to understand your words?"

The Being said, "I am your Maker from the realm of Ooranos, another dimension, and you are the first Adam. I made your body from the dust of the ground[8] and from my Spirit I breathed into you the gift of life. You are man, made in our image, the very image of God."

Adam thought to himself, *What a wonderful feeling to have life! Is there any gift like this gift?* He had no understanding of the fullness of this gift, but he did realize it was something very wonderful.

The Creator, knowing his thoughts said, "Yes, life is the most wonderful gift one could ever receive. But not only that, your life has been fashioned after the image and likeness of your Creator. You are the physical expression of our love, grace, and glory in this creation."

"Are all the other creatures I see around us also made in God's image?"[9]

"No, all these creatures were made for your pleasure. You are not to refer to yourself as a creature because you are a man, made in the image and likeness of God.[10] As a man, you are much different from the creatures. Creatures were not made in the image and likeness of their Creator, but each one was made for your pleasure[11] and each will reproduce after their own kind."

"Lord, I don't fully understand. If I am called man and made after your image and likeness, then what are you?"

"I am your Creator, I am called, the Word of God who is the Divine Expression[12] of my Father in heaven who is love, a life-giving Spirit who is from everlasting to everlasting. My Father and I are one. Because we are Love, we desired to make a man-child in our image so that we could express our love to him and that he could also experience that same love within himself. Our desire is to give you all things pertaining to life and God likeness.[13] You will share our joy and peace in this garden, but the greatest thing is that we will share in the communion of fellowship as one family together."

"You gave me understanding of many words and things, Lord, but I do not understand these things, or the word *love*. Would you help me to understand?"

"I AM. I am Love because I come from the Father. I AM is your Abba Father, who is Love. I AM is your Comforter, the Spirit of Life, and He too is Love. I AM the Eternal Son of my Father, and we exist in union with the Spirit of God, and we are one God. Love exists only because we exist in family relationship as three, yet we are one. To understand this and its meaning is to understand our glory, the glory that you share and why you were created.

"Now concerning love, it can only be understood by time, time spent with me. You are the greatest idea that was ever devised in the mind of your Abba, your Papa. You can call me Love because I AM God, and God is Love."

Adam said, "Can I see my Father who is in Ooranos?"

"In seeing me, Adam, you have seen your Father."

Then Love gently pulled Adam into His arms and embraced him. He said, "Adam, I love you, and my love will never fail you, trust me always." A rush of emotions that he could not explain filled his soul. It was like a waterfall of pure joy flowing over him. There was a warm radiance of light coming from Love's innermost being that enveloped Adam like a coat. The light did not hurt his eyes, yet it blinded him to everything else that was around him.[14] It was as if he had meshed with Love and became one spirit with Him. It gave him the assurance that this was where he belonged and what he would forever long for.[15]

Adam thought to himself, *This wonderful feeling... this must be love.*

Love, once again knowing his thoughts, said, "Adam, love is much more than just a word or a feeling. True love is an expression, the expression of God in and through you."

"How is it that you even know my thoughts, Lord?"

"I know everything about you, Adam, even the number of hairs on your head at any moment in time. Even when I am not here in your presence, the Holy Spirit of God resides with you, and your thoughts never leave the hearing of my heart. I love to hear the thoughts of your heart and mind, for in that sense we are one."

Adam would look back many times in his life and remember his first embrace, for no other experience in life would equal that moment. Nor would he be able to explain it in words, but would spend the rest of his life trying to understand so that he would come to know the true meaning of Love.

"Come, Adam, let me show you through the Paradise I have created for you."

Then Love took Adam by the hand and began to walk with him in the cool of the morning to show him many of the wonders of the beautiful garden that was before him.

Chapter 2

The Garden

God planted the garden of Eden in the southeastern region of the land of Eden. The garden was a paradise where every need was provided for man to enjoy, but most importantly, the garden was where man and God met and enjoyed communion together. The garden itself was by the wisdom and plan of God to become a metaphor of the future relationship between God and the children of God. The children would be called *The Garden of God*,[16] and God would come down to his garden and gather lilies there.

Love said, "Adam, you have been created and placed in this garden paradise, and you will find pleasure in tending it and partaking of all its fruits. But not only this, you will go into the entire world where you are given dominion and authority over all living things. You and all your posterity are to oversee this world and keep everything in order. You are to care for all the birds, the animals, and the fish of the sea, for they are all here to serve you and bring pleasure to you.

"It took me five days to create all that you see around you, both in the heavens and upon on the earth. But on this, the sixth day, I created the crowning glory of all this creation, and that crowning glory is you.[17] So tomorrow we will together celebrate because I will declare it my day of rest. I will come and establish you in My rest[18] and each seventh day will remind you of your rest in me, for in me you shall have no lack."

"What is so special about the number seven, Lord?"

"The number seven is my number of perfect completeness. When I refer to something with the number seven, it not only speaks of completeness, but absolute perfection.[19]

"Here is something for you to think about. One year is determined by one revolution of the earth around the sun. One month is determined by one revolution of the moon around the earth. One day is determined by one revolution of the earth on its axis. But one week will be determined only by my rest. By my word is the seven-day week established." And Love instructed Adam on many other such things.

Adam began to understand the magnificent power and wisdom of the God who was holding his hand. He felt the wonders of his person and the glory of this magnificent Being as he contemplated the splendor of the creation around him. The beautiful green grass, plants, and flowers were each as unique in appearance as was the sweet aroma that filled the air around them. He picked fruits and nuts and vegetables of all sorts, intuitively naming each one after its unique flavor. He thought, *Wow, life has so much variety! I am so blessed and thankful to be here experiencing this gift of life and the wonders of my Abba's world.*

His mind was overwhelmed with the power and beauty of it all. The garden was not only graced with every kind of delicious fruit and flower, but beautiful mountains with majestic waterfalls lined the horizon and crystal-clear rivers flowed through the land from east to west. Everywhere he turned, there was such a variety of life that he didn't even notice that he had let go of Love's hand and was running, leaping, and dancing in circles of joy and shouting praises of thanksgiving.

Then suddenly, the euphoria of the moment was interrupted as Adam saw a large, silky black creature running toward him. Before he could react, the creature leaped into the air and hit Adam in the chest, sending him flying backward onto the ground. The creature pounced on top of Adam, and with its tail switching and with what looked like a smile on its face, the creature began to lick Adam's face with its big, wet tongue. The creature then jumped into the air, spun in a circle, and landed about five feet from Adam who was still in a state of surprise.

The creature was now poised in a pouncing position with head down, tail switching in the air, and tongue panting with excitement. Adam now realized that the creature wanted to play. He began to laugh and lunged at the creature only to be outmaneuvered by the quick reflexes of the animal. Adam flew past the creature and over an embankment into the cool river with a big splash. He was so startled from the cool water that he bolted back onto dry ground as if he had wings. As he stood there dripping, he did not know whether to cry or laugh, that is until he glanced over to see Love laughing.

Love said, "You should see the look on your face."

Adam burst out into uncontrollable laughter. He bent over holding his abdomen with both hands and fell to the ground in a fetal position. He laughed so hard and long that his ribs hurt. He said, "Lord, I have to stop laughing! My side hurts!"

Love smiled as he replied, "Soon one of those ribs in your side is going to be a source of great joy for you."

That night, Adam would ponder the meaning of this statement.

After gaining his composure, Adam asked what the creature that played with him was called. Love replied, "Whatever you want to call him is up to you. Just as you gave names to the fruits that you have been eating, do the same with the living creatures around you. It is for man to name all the creatures in this world, and whatever you decide to call them is what their names shall be."

This excited Adam, and he said, "I will call that creature a panther," meaning in his language, *the sweet influence of God.* "He is much like you, Lord. He has both a sweet spirit and a coat that shines with such brilliance, like a reflection on the water." After that he spent the rest of his day naming many of the animals in the garden.

As the sun was disappearing over the mountains, Love said to Adam, "I am going now, but I will return in the morning, and we will spend another day together. It will be the seventh day, and we will celebrate my day of rest. I also have something very important to tell you. In the meantime, do not go from this spot in the garden, but sleep here."

Adam lay down and fell asleep, marveling over all that he had experienced during the first day of his life.

As the sun goes down in Paradise, Adam would sleep in the soft grass under a small tree, with perfect health, in a perfect environment, with perfect temperature. God created the perfect environment for man.

Chapter 3

The Tree

As the morning light began to break over the mountains, Adam was awakened to a symphony of song. Birds of every variety and color were singing and making melody, which caused his soul to sing. The aroma of the flowers around him delighted his sense of smell. The blanket of warm dew that filled the garden felt good on his skin.

The earth in that day was watered by a mist in the morning, for there was no such thing as rain then. A water belt surrounded the earth, blocking harmful rays from the sun. Later in man's history, this water belt would fall, creating a flood, and at that time, the lifespan of man would sharply decrease.

Adam's senses began to fill him with joyful anticipation of experiencing another day in the garden. As he was lying there waiting for his body to fully awaken from sleepiness, he noticed that something heavy was resting on his abdomen. Looking down, it was the playful panther, who found that Adam's abdomen made a soft and warm place to lay his head. As Adam stroked the silky soft head of the panther, he said, "I am going to give you a personal name. I will call you *Shachar.*" The animal seemed to understand what Adam had said and responded with a purring sound that Adam found very soothing.

Suddenly a voice said, "Adam! Come over here. I have prepared something for you to eat from the fruits of the garden."

"Lord, it's you!" Adam jumped up and ran over to Love, who with open arms greeted him with a loving embrace. Once again Adam experienced wonderful feelings of ecstasy, peace, and tranquility that filled him from head to foot. And, just like the first embrace he had experienced the day prior, he did not want to let go of the glory that enveloped him.

Then Love said, "Come, Adam, sit down and let us share a covenant meal together.[20] I have prepared fruit and something special for you called bread. It is made from the grains of the fields. And also honey, which is created by little flying creatures, which you need to name."

Adam said, "Then I will call them Honey Bees." And that has been their name ever since.

Then Love put the honey on the bread and held it up and said; "Adam, I want you to know that your Father and I love you and that our love will never, never, ever fail you. For as long as you abide in our love, you will have life. This bread represents my promise of life to you, and the honey is the sweetness of our love and affection for you. I am the giver and sustainer of your life, so believe and trust in me. My divine influence will guide your heart, and you will be a reflection of that life if you abide in my love. I also give you this promise. You will have complete rule and authority over the entire earth that I have created for you, as long as you abide in my love. Let this be an everlasting covenant between us, for today will be your completion."[21]

As Adam and Love broke bread together, Love instructed him in many other things and shared with him many more secrets of the earth and of the universe that filled the heavens above.

"Love, how was all this creation brought forth?"

"I am the Word of God, and from the beginning I was with God because I am God. Everything that was created was brought forth by my word.[22] All that was conceived in the heart of my Father, I spoke into existence. This garden that you are in is the center of this world, and this world is the center of the universe that you see above you at night. The universe is ever expanding outward and will continue to grow larger, and for each star that is born, I give it a name. It was all created for man's enjoyment, so that they might marvel in the glory of their Creator."

"Lord, you said yesterday that you had something very important to tell me this day. Is this important thing something other than what you have already shared with me?"

Love rose up and said, "Come, follow me, Adam."

They talked for a long time while going through the garden. Along the way, Adam continued to give names to all the different animals they encountered. Adam said, "Look at this one, Lord; I am going to call him a horse."

"That is a perfect name for that creature. He can run like the wind, and you will enjoy riding on him, for he is both strong and gentle. With his great strength, he can carry you through valleys, over great mountains and vast plains, so that you will not tire along the way."

Then they arrived at the center of the garden, and Love said, "Do you see the tree standing before you that is in the center of this garden?"

"Yes, Lord."

"This tree is the Tree of the Knowledge of Good and Evil. From all the trees in this garden, you may freely eat, but of this tree, I warn you, you shall not eat of its fruit. For in the day that you eat the fruit of this tree, you will have broken covenant with me, and you will surely die.

Your spiritual connection with me will die, and in time, even your physical body will also die. Remember when I told you that love had to be learned?"

"Yes, Lord. But what is the knowledge of good and evil? Is not everything good?"

The LORD God commanded the man, saying, "From any tree of the garden you may eat freely; but from the tree of the knowledge of good and evil you shall not eat, for in the day that you eat from it you will surely die."

Genesis 2:16-17

"Adam, it is true that everything in itself is good, but it is not for man to decide what is good or what is evil. It is better for you not to know these things, for this is reserved only for God. Only God knows good and evil because God knows what is truly good and God cannot be tempted by evil. However, if man considers good and evil, he can be tempted by both. This is why it is better for man not to know good or evil but rather to abide with me and hear my voice, for in me all truth resides.

"I will abide with you, and you will abide with me, but if you are separated from me through spiritual death, then you will be controlled by the dark force of sin and death and no longer listen to my voice. Nor would you any longer realize your true identity, destiny, and purpose.

"I am your Creator, and I am your life, and as long as you trust and listen to me, then you will have life and peace. Again I warn you, this tree stands for all that is harmful and is void of life with Me. Eat rather from the Tree of Life, which is in another place in this garden that I will show you at another time. In that tree is life eternal and peace in me. This tree however, is trust in self, the created, and not in me, your Creator.

"Again I ask, do you remember when I told you that love must be learned?"

"Yes, Lord."

"Love is also a choice. To truly love as I love you, you must choose to love in spite of your feelings. If you love my word and trust my voice, then you will demonstrate that you love me. As I told you before, you are not like all the other creatures in the garden; you have been given free will. You can choose to trust me, or not to trust me. If you choose to love me and not eat from the Tree of the Knowledge of Good and Evil, I will know that you love me, and you will have eternal life.

"You see, Adam, true love is proven by choice. It is first, to trust me with all your heart, and second, to choose the highest good of someone else above that of yourself. My Father and I in heaven have chosen to love you, and our love will never fail. If you will believe and trust in me and my word, you will remain in life and peace. This is love; to believe me, to trust in me, and to obey my voice, for I am Love."

"I think I am beginning to understand, Lord. It seems that love is the most important thing that we can know and express to one another. The love that you and Abba share for one another is like the love that you and I share for one another."

"Yes, Adam, true love is of God, and to love me is to love Abba, for we are one.

"But know this; there are four kinds of love. God's love is sacrificial love. This love goes to the extent of even giving one's own life for another; it gives with no thought of anything in return. Then there is love of respect, which is to respect all others for who they are, not what they do. There are also two other kinds of love. These two loves are a special love for one's own family members, a special closeness that others outside that family cannot share in, but only within their own families.

"Adam, every time that my truth is awakened in your spirit, you will then see others embraced with love."

"Love, will I someday have a family that I can love?"

"Adam, do you remember what I told you about the number seven?"

"Yes, Lord. You said, "The number seven is your number of perfect completeness, and it not only speaks of completeness, but absolute perfection."

"That is correct, and so because today is my seventh day, you will be made complete and perfect. I will bring forth that perfection that will complete you from what resides within you. From you, she will enter into my rest."[23]

"She, Lord? I don't understand."

Chapter 4

The Woman

Love said, "Adam, it's not good for you to be alone in the garden, so today I have a special surprise for you. When my Father and I created you a man, we made you both male and female. So today, as I promised you when your rib hurt from laughing, I am going to bless you by taking one of your ribs, and from it I will make you an equal."

Before Adam had a chance to respond with even a word, Love touched Adam's cheek with His hand, and Adam fell instantly to the ground, slipping into a deep sleep. As Adam slept, he had a dream. In his dream he saw the moon, and the moon turned into a crystal-like ball. The sun went behind the moon, and as the sunlight pierced through the crystal moon, multicolored beams of light were shooting into the heavens and creating thousands and thousands of beautiful stars, stars of many colors.

While Adam was dreaming, Love removed one of his ribs and fashioned from it another man in female form.[24] No earthly creation was ever created by Love more beautiful than this. Adam's outward form was a reflection of God's glory in powerful strength and dignity, but this new female creation reflected like nothing else in all the world the majestic splendor, beauty, and glory of man.[25]

No animal, mountain scene, sunset, or even the stars of heaven would equal the beauty of the woman brought forth from man. She was what had been hidden in the man until now, a beauty in all creation that had no equal. She was the crowning glory of man.

After creating the woman's body, Love breathed into her the breath of life, just as he had done with Adam. And the woman became a living soul. Love stood behind her as she came to life. She slowly rose up, leaning upon her arms with one knee bent, trying to open her eyes to the bright light of the day. As she was able to stop squinting and focus, the first thing she saw was the body of Adam lying in front of her. Somewhat puzzled, she gazed at him and the environment of the beautiful flowers and trees that surrounded him. She thought, *My, how beautiful.*

Then Love said, "Yes, but far more beautiful are you."

Startled, she turned quickly rising to her knees and replied, "Who are you, my Lord?"

"I am your Maker, I am Love. I created you from the man's side and breathed into you the breath of life. It was not good for the man to be alone, so you were brought forth from the man for completion, and to become his companion. The two of you were created for love and intimacy, and you will become as one."

"What does that mean, *that we shall be as one?*"

"You and the man were created in the image and likeness of your Creator. Soon you will come together with this man, and you will become one flesh through the birth of a child. This triangle will be a reflection of what we are like. Adam will become a father, you will become a mother, and your child will be the result of your love together. Likewise, your Father God, who is in Ooranos, is also My Father, and even though there is no male and female in Ooranos, the Holy Spirit of God is like a mother to you and all creation, and I am God's Son, and we are Love. The difference is that we are eternally one God, not three. This will always be a mystery to you, but you will know us through knowing me, for if you see me, you see the Father, and the Spirit will always comfort you when I am not here."

Then Love said, "Let me hide you from Adam behind these trees by the river, then I will bring you to him when he awakens. And while you wait, you might find a flower that pleases you that you could place in your hair."[26]

While the woman was hidden from the presence of the man, she was still somewhat puzzled as to what was happening. She was experiencing sudden life with little explanation or information coming from Love, as he had done with Adam. She felt confused, but yet had an assurance of well-being and joy within her soul.

She began to marvel at the creation around her, and even though she had just come to life, she instinctively understood so much about the environment. This was because God had created the man and the woman's body at a certain maturity already with age and imputed knowledge.

The earth also was created from the beginning with certain maturity and signs of great age.[27] There were giant trees that already stood hundreds of feet high and minerals in the ground like gold, silver, and diamonds that were produced by great pressure during the creation. This reality would become a stumbling block to the understanding of many men in the centuries to come.

As the woman was instructed, she began to look for a flower to put in her hair. There was a variety around her, but she chose a large white one that would later be named *the lily*. As she placed the lily in her hair, she looked down into a still pool of water that was next to her and noticed she could see herself in the water. This pleased her, and she instinctively began to adjust the flower and her hair, until she was satisfied with the reflection that looked back at her.

After several hours of sleep, Adam awakened and noticed a slight twinge of pain in his side. As he examined it, he noticed a long red mark in his skin where the rib had been removed. He would carry this mark for the rest of his life to remind him of God's gift to him, the bride that was taken out of his side. Adam was unaware that centuries from this time, another Adam would come. He would be the last Adam and would bear a similar wound in his side. And out of his side would come his bride, that which was hidden in God.

As Adam stood to his feet, Love said, "How do you feel, Adam?"

"I am well, Lord, but what just happened? I must have slept for some time, and when I awoke I noticed this red mark on my side with a slight twinge of pain."

"Let me show you what happened."

Love then brought the woman out from behind the trees of the garden to Adam.

As the woman stood before the man, Adam suddenly became speechless. He stood there for a moment trying to gather his thoughts. The only thing he was able to articulate was, "Wow!" His heart began to pound, his face flushed red, and his emotions were running wild. He stood there dumbfounded for the longest time, until Love's voice broke the silence.

"Well, Adam, what do you think? I made her from one of your ribs. Not bad for a spare rib, yes?"

Adam, still unable to speak, just took in the beauty of the woman. Her hair flowed over her shoulders and down to her waist as the sun made it shimmer and dance with sparkles against her light brown skin. Her form was like the beauty of the mountain ranges that rose up from the grassy plains to the west of the garden, and smooth like the glassy river that flowed through the middle of the garden. But still, all Adam was able to say was, "Wow!"

Once again, Love said, "Adam, what do you think?!"

"I think she is flesh of my flesh and bone of my bone, so I will call her *woman*, because she was created out of my side." He would later name her Eve, meaning, *the mother of all living.*

"Yes, Adam, this gift, which was hidden in you, proceeded out of the wound in your side. I brought her out from your side to signify that she is to be your equal. Yet, because she is not as strong as you physically, she shall live secure under the strong arm of your protection. Both of you are incomplete without the other, but together you will now be one flesh, and you will now begin to understand even more the meaning of love."

Then Love said to the woman, "And what are your thoughts, woman?"

"I am so very thankful, my Lord, and even though I am not fully understanding everything yet, I sense an overwhelming joy in my soul. My only desire is to be well pleasing to you and to the man that you created me from. May he find me well pleasing."

Then Adam replied, "I am very pleased. And I will love you with the kind of love that I have been learning from our Creator, for now I will truly learn what love means."

Adam reached out and took the woman's hand. He said, "May I embrace you as Love embraced me when I was first brought forth?"

"Yes, of course, that would please me very much."

As Adam pulled his wife into his arms and their bodies met, he was not expecting the sensations that met him there. Time seem to suddenly stand still for both him and the woman. They felt as if they had stepped through a doorway into another world, a world of silence, except for a language of the senses that filled their minds and hearts with loving thoughts. They became so lost in the moment they were oblivious to everything else around them. That is until Love's voice broke the silence, which brought them back to the world.

He said, "I am going to leave you now, but before I go I want to give you my blessing."

"Love, before you bless us, would you tell me what is the meaning of a dream I had while sleeping?"

"Yes, tell me, what was your dream?"

"I dreamt that the moon was a crystal ball, and the sun was behind the moon, and as the sun's rays came through the moon, spears of many colors shot into the heavens creating many beautiful stars."

Love said, "The sun is you, Adam, and the moon is your wife. The stars will be the many races of men who come from your loins. So now come together, be fruitful and multiply, and fill the earth. No one will ever have more descendants than you, Adam, for you are the first man."

Then Love put his hands upon their heads and blessed them, and said to them, "Be fruitful and multiply, and fill the earth, and subdue it; and rule over the fish of the sea and over the birds of the sky and over every living thing that moves on the earth. Behold, I have given you every plant yielding seed that is on the surface of all the earth, and every tree, which has fruit yielding seed; it shall be food for you; and to every beast of the earth and to every bird of the sky and to everything that moves on the earth, which has life. I have given you every green plant for food. Now, look long at all that I have created, both in the heavens and upon the earth, be astonished, wonder with amazement, for all this was created for my pleasure and yours, and it is very good.

"Adam, now take your wife's hand, and show her the paradise I have made for the both of you. Tend it and arrange its beauty to your liking. Also, keep in mind the warning I earlier gave to you, for you lack nothing."

Adam shows Eve the garden of paradise that the Lord God created.

And Adam took his wife's hand and began to show her all the wonders of the garden, and everything was only good.

The Dark Force Emerges

When God created the heavens and the earth, there was a multitude of heavenly beings watching from Ooranos and marveling at the power and majesty of God. However, there was one being that was not rejoicing over God's generosity to His newly created man. And from the realm of Ooranos, he was watching intently, but at a distance.

This being was a magnificent creature and was a leader of many other angels that served and ministered to God. Originally he was called by the name Lucifer and served God as one of His most influential and trusted servants. Because of his great beauty and power, pride and jealousy crept in, and he became corrupt and deceptive. As time went on, he became narcissistic, even believing he was as powerful as his Creator.

Because God created all that was created for man, envy and jealousy began to capture Lucifer's heart. God had made a man in his own image and made him lord over the entire earth. So Lucifer began to plot how he would take over this new creation and become its ruler and become like God. He thought to himself, *I will be like the Most High, and I will sit on the throne to rule over earth and its heavens, and I will destroy anyone who will not serve me.*

The sad part of this transformation in Lucifer was that God had given more power and beauty to him than any of the other angels. Lucifer had musical instruments built into his body, and was able to create great symphonies of music for all of Ooranos. He would perform before God and for the enjoyment of many others who lived in the heavenly realm.

Many to this day wonder why an angel who was given so much was not satisfied with all the blessings and prestige that he was afforded by his Creator. But instead, he had to have more. When one asks, "Where did evil come from?" we have to conclude that it was birthed within the heart of this being, Lucifer.[28]

One day God called Lucifer before Him and said, "I want you to watch over man in the garden and be a minister unto them."[29]

Lucifer immediately thought, *This is my opportunity.* The evil that was birthing in his heart now began to take control of his reason. He knew that he could never overthrow God's throne by a direct confrontation in Ooranos, the realm of the spiritual, so he began to secretly plan a deception whereby he could legally have the authority that was given to man transferred to him.

Lucifer had many angels under his command, and many of them were also deceived into thinking that this plan could actually succeed.

He called a meeting with a certain group of them, those who he had authority and influence over. He said to them, "Here is my plan. The Most High has made a covenant with the man. He has told the man not to eat from the Tree of the Knowledge of Good and Evil. If he eats from the Tree and breaks the covenant, then the sentence of death and separation from the Most High will come upon him. Man will then become weak; he will no longer trust God, and he will separate himself from God because he will now consider God his enemy. However, because of the promise of God, man will still have rule over the creation. We will then be able to rule the creation through and in the man. The title deed to the whole creation will become ours and he will become enslaved to us."[30]

Many of the angels bought the lie from this father of lies. Their hearts too were affected by the powerful force of sin and darkness to believe that they would become gods, even one day becoming like the Most High himself.

Lucifer said, "Those of you who join me, I will make you rulers over the kingdoms of the earth. We will control men to do our will and bring their race to destruction."

Sin's power transformed these angels of light into demons of darkness. They began to chant, "Great is Lucifer, who is like the Most High God."

Chapter 6

The Temptation

Adam shared Eve's first day of life by showing her all the wonders of the paradise that Love had made for them. He also showed her the tree in the center of the garden and explained the warning that had given to him, that they were not to eat the fruit from that tree, for if they did they would surely die.

As they spent this time getting to know one another, Adam held on to Eve's hand almost the entire time they were together. He thought, *This is too wonderful to be*

real. It must be a dream. If I let go of her hand, I might awaken and she will have disappeared.

He said, "My wife, you are the most beautiful being in all creation; you are surely the crowning glory of all that Love created. How did Love ever come up with such an idea as you? I am so overwhelmed with love for you that it is hard for me to concentrate on anything else."

"I too feel the same, my husband. Maybe we feel this way because our Creator knows this kind of love within himself."

"Yes, my love, that must be it. He told me that we were made in His image and likeness. He too must possess this love within Himself, for He said, 'I am one God, and God is Love'. Yet he referred to himself in the plural, meaning two or more distinct persons.[31]

"If God was alone by Himself, He would not know love, would He? In order to know love, there must be someone else to love. He said to me that our Father in heaven is God, and that God was Love, and yet, that He himself was God. He called himself the *Word of God* and said that I could call him Love. And then there was the Spirit of God, who He said was to be our Comforter. When I asked

45

Him if I could see our Father God, He said, 'If you have seen me, you have seen the Father.' I have marveled at and pondered these things much."

Eve said, "He also spoke to me about similar things while you were sleeping. What a wonderful and awesome Father we have. He gave us two wonderful gifts, the gift of life and the gift of knowing and experiencing this love with Him and each other."

During the rest of the day, they playfully ran through the garden and splashed in the crystal-clear stream that ran through the garden's center. They enjoyed being together, discovering new things, and giving names to all the animals, according to their uniqueness.

There was one special bird that followed them everywhere, even at times landing on Adam's head or shoulder. When Adam sat down, the bird would sit on his knee. It was a very colorful creature, and Adam could not decide what to name him.

One afternoon, the couple sat down in the grass, and as usual the bird landed on Adam's knee. Eve said, "Adam what are you going to name this feathered friend of yours?"

Adam looked at the bird and said, "What shall I call you?"

Suddenly the bird spoke back to Adam and said, "What shall I call you?"

Adam and Eve burst into laughter. Adam said as he laughed, "What shall you call me? you silly bird, you aren't naming me, I'm naming you!

"How about that, Eve? a bird that talks."

"Yes, our Lord has a sense of humor, doesn't he? Why don't you call him a parrot, Adam?" which meant in their language *talking bird*!

Then, as the end of a perfect day was coming to a close and the sunlight was giving way to the evening skies, Adam and Eve looked into each other's eyes. Something amazing and wonderful was happening. Loving emotions of passion began to awaken in them. Instinctively they brought their lips together to experience their first kiss. As one kiss led to another, they fell onto the soft grass beneath them and became intimate for the first time.[32]

Only in this paradise state would man ever be able to experience the kind of intimacy that they experienced, for it was coupled with both the pure expressions of physical love, and the complete innocence of mind and heart. It was the way God intended man and woman to experience this act of intimacy. It was an appreciation for one another, an unselfish gift of giving one to the other.

As the days passed, Adam and Eve continued to be naked without any shame. Every day was a new adventure of discovering all the wonders in the garden, and every night was full of loving passion as they continued to grow more deeply in love with each other.

The variety of animals continually amazed them, and the variety of fruits to eat was beyond imagination. Even after the sun went down, the adventure continued as they would lie in the soft grass, look up at the heavens, and marvel at the stars shining like diamonds, sometimes shooting like firebrands from one horizon to the other. It was on one of these peaceful nights that unbeknown to Adam and Eve, their paradise would be invaded.

On this night, Adam had fallen asleep, but Eve lay awake still looking at the stars when suddenly she heard a voice calling to her from the center of the garden. The voice softly called, "Woman, come here." She quickly rose up and walked toward the voice. As she got closer, she could see that there was a luminous glow coming from the tree in the center of the garden. There was something or someone in the tree that was giving off the glow. At first, she thought with excitement that Love had come for a visit, but after getting close enough, she realized that this was not Love but an animal, the most beautiful animal she had ever seen, and the animal even spoke in a language that she understood.

Eve could now see the outline of the animal. Its coat glowed in the dark with stripes of many colors. Unknown to her, the creature was called a serpent, and the angel Lucifer had entered into the serpent. He was an evil angel but came to her as an angel of light.

The Serpent said with a soft voice, "Hello, woman."

Eve was so excited to make this new friend. "Hello. I have never met anyone like you in the garden. Who are you, and how is it that you speak words like Adam and I do?"

"I have been sent by God to be your friend. Would you like to be my friend?"

"Oh yes!" said Eve.

"Well then, let us covenant together by having some of this tasty fruit. It will be a symbol of our friendship."

Eve recoiled and stepped back slightly and said, "Oh no, for God said that we may eat the fruit from any of the trees in the garden, but from this tree in the middle of the garden we are not to eat from it or even touch it, or we will die."

The Serpent then said with a slight snicker, "You surely won't die. The reason that God told you not to eat from this tree is because in the day you eat the fruit of this tree, your eyes of understanding will be opened, and you will be like God, knowing good and evil."

As Eve was thinking about what the Serpent said, he once again brought her attention to the fruit.

"Look at this fruit, woman. Is not this fruit more desirable than any other fruit in this garden?"[33]

Then Eve thought to herself, *It does look good, and it surely must taste better than any other fruit in the garden.*

This was Lucifer's first temptation. Knowing man had appetites of the body, like hunger, he would tempt her with what would later become known as *the lust of the flesh.*

Again, Eve thought, *The fruit is so beautiful and such a delight to the eyes. I really would like to feel and touch and possess it.*

This temptation would later become man's insatiable appetite and desire for money and material things. It would be called *the lust of the eyes.*

Finally, Eve said to herself, *If I eat this fruit, I will be just like God,* not realizing that she was already like God, for she had been made in his image.

This temptation would become man's lust for power and would become known as *the pride of life*.

Then she reached up and picked the fruit. She stood there for a moment, gazing at its beauty, and then took a bite. The fruit was sweet at first, but then a bitter aftertaste filled her mouth. She took another bite and again it was sweet, so she picked another piece and ran back to where Adam was lying. "Adam," she said. "Wake up! Look what I have brought you."

Adam awoke from a deep sleep and asked her what she had. Eve said, "I have a piece of fruit for you. It is from the tree in the middle of the garden. The Serpent said that if we ate the fruit, we would become like God!"

Fear shot through Adam's soul. He said, "Woman! What have you done? You know what Love said to me, that if we ate the fruit we would surely die!"

"No, Adam, the animal spoke to me and said that God did not want us to eat it because he knew that we would become like he is. And look, I have eaten, and I am not dead. Please, Adam, have some. It is very good."

Adam knew that the opposite was true, that the woman that God gave to him, and that he loved so much, was about to die. Adam felt a sickness in his stomach and a pain in his heart. Tears filled his eyes at the thought of losing the love of his life. Then he said to himself, *She is flesh of my flesh and bone of my bone. If she dies, then I will also die with her.* He said to her, "Woman, give me the fruit." And he ate it.

The dark force of sin immediately began to work within them. Like a virus, it was transferred from Lucifer to Eve and from Eve to Adam and would now be passed on from one generation to the next, infecting every human being from conception to death. This sin of the one man brought death to all men.

No rest came to Adam and his wife for the remainder of that night. Nightmares and frightening dreams filled their sleep, and when dawn's light began to fill the sky, they lay there staring at each other and not able to speak. Eve's eyes were full of tears, and her heart was full of regret. She thought, *I wish I could undue what I have done, but it is like throwing a stone into the river, once I let go of the stone, I can not get it back.*

She clung to Adam in confusion and fear, wondering what would now become of them.

Chapter 7

The Accusers

Lucifer then left the garden and went before God to give Him a report. God said to Lucifer, "Have you been watching over man in the garden as I have commanded you?"[34]

"Yes, my Lord, and I have come to report that the man has broken your law, the commandment that he should not eat from the tree in the center of the garden. I myself was there and saw the very act."

Lucifer knew that the Tree of the Knowledge of Good and Evil would rob man of his innocence and bring him into sin consciousness. Once mankind was living under law-based sin consciousness, Lucifer would forever have a case to accuse the man before God. Under sin's power, man would feel condemned by God and would strive to please or appease God through a law-based mentality: do good-get good, do bad-get bad. This then would become the power of sin and condemnation,[35] the power of *the Tree*.

The Tree, which was the mother of the expanded law later to be given on Mount Sinai, would accuse the man's conscience, causing his sin to increase. An unhealthy fear of God would increase, and natural man would mistrust God's intentions. In addition to the accusations to man's own conscience, Lucifer would continually accuse man before God using the law.

Lucifer's lie brought the death blow that would cause man's spiritual relationship with God to die. And now, man, living by human intellect alone, or humanism, would be blinded by his narcissistic ideas and philosophies. Instead of looking for that loving embrace that God desires to give all men, he instead would run to embrace his own gods, who would feed his sinful lusts.

In darkness to the truth, man would create for himself idols, loving the creation instead of the Creator. Even those who would come to know the truth and believe in the living God would tend to approach Him through the law, not love, through religion, not personal relationship.

Sin's power would cause man to separate himself from God. He would embrace the lie, listen to the voices of his accusers, and mistrust the voice of his Creator. He would lose the ability to understand and comprehend the true nature of his origin, birthright, and identity. Thus, mankind would entertain shame and guilt and try to appeal to God's mercy through good works and religious exercise.

Then the Lord said to Lucifer, "So you have come before me to-what? Accuse the man?"

Lucifer said, "Did he not sin, and did he not break your law? Let your law accuse him!" Then he left the presence of the Lord.

Lucifer then gathered the angels that were following him and said, "Our plan is working, and now man will view the Most High with suspicion and no longer trust Him, but fear and reject Him. Now we will rule over him, and his world will become ours. The man has made a covenant with me, and I will now bring my claim of legal ownership before the Most High. We shall rule. Any who oppose us, we will destroy!"

All the angels began to cheer and chant, "Hail Lucifer, for he has triumphed over the Most High God!"

As Lucifer and his legions were celebrating, Michael the Archangel came before the Lord and said, "My Lord and my God, evil has filled the angel Lucifer's heart, and there is a rebellion forming. Should I gather my forces to wage war with them so that they might be cast out from Ooranos?"

"No, Michael, not at this time. Lucifer has become a fool and embraced the dark force of evil, so we will give him enough time to show himself to be the fool he is before all heaven and earth, and then he will be cast out. In the meantime there will be a place prepared for him and his followers."

Then Michael said, "Praise be to you my Lord, holy and righteous are you, for all men shall see your great wisdom and glory when this Evil One is cast down!"

After this, the family of God met. Father said, "Evil has now consumed Lucifer's heart and has caused the man to fall from the glory and identity that we created him for. Man has become like one of us, knowing good and evil. He will now live from the knowledge of the Tree of Good and Evil, determining what is good and what is evil, what is moral and what is immoral, what is right and what is wrong according to his own natural mind of reason and not ours. For he will only know the thoughts of man according to the spirit of man, and he will not know our mind until the time determined.

"Until that time, man will mistrust our intentions and question our love for him. The power of the Tree will become the law of sin and condemnation to him, and the accusations of Lucifer will cause him to judge by it and not by our Word. Knowledge he will gain, but wisdom he will lack. He will now view us as angry and condemning, and forever try to appease this imagined hate and anger, all according to the knowledge of good and evil."

"Father, I know it is in our plan that man would become one with us, but it is so painful to see what they must suffer in order to achieve this."

"Son, it is more painful to see what you must suffer in order to achieve this. You know that man is predestined to choose. Some will choose death; some will choose life. We cannot interfere with his free will. The destiny of many, by their own choice, will lead them to live without boundaries; they will by choice bring death and destruction upon themselves. However, we shall fence in the boundaries of our elected ones. The fenced-in boundaries of their destiny will be to become one with us through the persuasion of our divine influence upon their hearts. Through your gift, they will receive our grace and our faith to believe, and then they will truly be one with us in Love."

"Yes, and I will teach them all things and show them all wisdom, and I will comfort them in their distress. For I will live in them, nurture them, and care for them."

"Yes, Father, and I will give whatever it takes to redeem them, even my very life."

"So shall it be. Until we redeem man through the Way, two others will continue to accuse him: the law condemning his conscience, and Lucifer, accusing him before us and to man himself continually. Many will suffer by their own choice. Man must come to understand the seriousness of sin's consequences; he must choose life or death, the beautiful over the worthless.

"Now, let us send man from the garden and block the way to the Tree of Life, lest he take and eat from the tree and live forever in this fallen state. As far as Lucifer goes, we shall use this Evil One for our purposes until we restore man to the glory and dignity that he was created for.

"Let us now go down to the garden and find the man."

Chapter 8

Mans First Religion

As the morning dawn was breaking, Adam rose up and thought to himself, *What will we do if Love comes to see us this morning?* Then, the woman stood up, and when Adam turned around and their eyes met, they looked at each other's nakedness and felt so ashamed; feelings they had never experienced before. Guilt's effect of disobeying Love produced heart wrenching pain within their souls. They had never had a second thought about being naked before.

Adam reached over and grabbed some leaves from a nearby fig tree, and with some small vines in his hands he said to Eve, "Let us make loin coverings for ourselves." This action came like an automatic reflex to the guilt and shame they felt. What Adam and Eve did not realize was that they invented what would become known as *religion, which would destroy the spiritual health of many, resulting in a distorted understanding or view of God.*[36]

As the morning sun broke through the darkness of the night past, fear was growing in Adam because he knew that Love would soon be coming to the garden.

Adam said to Eve, "The Lord will soon be coming and He told me that in the day that we ate from the tree we would die. So because we ate from the tree, He will surely kill us."

Eve's eyes began to flood with tears, and her troubled heart was vexed with painful sorrow. "Oh, husband, what can we do?"

Just then they heard someone walking in the garden. A voice called out, "Adam, where are you?"

Adam said, "It is the Lord! Quickly, we must find a place to hide."

Adam no longer referred to God as Love, for the power of sin had darkened his view of God. His only expectations were of judgment. He now viewed his Father as one full of anger and condemnation.

The voice had come from the east of the garden, so they ran to the west until they spotted a grove of myrtle trees, which provided a thick covering to hide in.

Ironically, and unknown to Adam and his wife, was the significance of the tree they had chosen to hide under. Its name in their language meant, *Behold the pathway to enter (life)*. The contrast of these leaves with the fig leaves that they were wearing was one of grace versus law or religion. A woman in the future would bear the same name, for she would find entrance into the King's saving presence through grace. Her name was Hadassah, meaning *Myrtle*, otherwise known as Esther.[37]

While the man and the woman shrank back in fear and shame from the presence of Love and wearing the leaves of religion, the true answer was above them. The leaves of the tree they hid under were crying out, "Behold the door, the door to forgiveness and life by grace."[38] Yet sin and fear now blinded the eyes of their hearts to any expectation of favor from their Creator. The only expectation they had was one of punishment and death. All humans today are born with this same expectation and mistrust of God because of the sin of the first Adam.

Once again they heard the voice of Love calling out, "Adam, where are you?" He was now much closer. As they cowered beneath the trees trembling, the sun broke over the peak of the mountains and began burning off the mist of the morning. Then they noticed that something was different. The garden was unusually quiet. The usual singing of the birds and animal sounds were absent. It was so quiet that the droplets of dew from the trees and plants falling to the ground sounded like thunder.

All creation was affected by the man's violation. Sin's presence in the garden even produced a spirit of fear in the animals. This caused even more anxiety in the couple.

Then they heard the footsteps of the Lord right outside of their hiding place, and for a third time the voice said, "Adam, where are you? Please come out, I Am Love and I am here to visit you."

Man's ears were now deaf to hear the statement, "I Am Love," for Satan had placed a blind over Adam and Eve's mind so that they would no longer believe that God loved them. All men would now be born this way. Only through spiritual rebirth could the blind be removed.

Eve then said to Adam, "Adam, what should we do? He knows we are here."

Adam said, "Yes, we must go out; perhaps He will not know that we ate from the tree."

As the man and the woman crawled out from their hiding place, they saw Love's feet standing before them. They did not dare look up to make eye contact with Him.

Then Love, testing them to see if they would tell the truth said, "Adam, why did you not answer me?"

With his head down and eyes to the ground Adam said, "When I heard your voice in the garden, I was afraid because I was naked, so I hid myself under these trees."[39]

Then Love said with a tender voice, "Who told you that you were naked? Did you eat from the tree that I warned you not to eat from?"

"Yes, Lord; the woman that you gave to me, she gave me the fruit, and I ate it."

Then Love with the same voice of compassion said to the woman, "Why did you do this?"

And the woman said, "The Serpent deceived me, Lord, so I ate it."

"Woman, it is true that the Serpent deceived you, but who really deceived you was my servant Lucifer, who entered the animal. I sent him here to watch over you both, but evil has captured his heart, and his desire now is to kill, steal, and destroy. From this day forward, he will be your enemy, and his desire will be to rule over you."

Love then said to Adam, "Adam, you both have spoken truthfully; however, it was not the woman who sinned, it was you. She was deceived because she was the weaker one.[40] You, however, received the command directly from me, yet you did not obey my voice, but listened to the voice of the Evil One speaking through your wife.

Remember, Adam? I told you that love was not just feelings but a choice. You listened to your feelings for your wife rather than to love me by choice. Emotions of love are good but they will fail. However, the choice to love in spite of emotions will never fail. Your wife would not have died as you feared, if you would have only chosen to love me first. Your accuser knew that he could not deceive you directly, so he got to you through your wife."

"Yes, Lord, the words that you speak are true. I should not have listened to the voice of the woman; I should have trusted you."

"You can still be reassured of my love, Adam, for that has not changed. I have not changed, nor will I ever change, for I Am the same yesterday, today, and forever. However, what has changed is your heart and understanding toward me. Because the power of sin has entered you, it will continually test you. Always remember though, I will never test you with sin or anything evil."

Chapter 9

The Curse

The Lord then turned to the Serpent, who was poised in a nearby tree, and said, "Because you have done this, deceived this woman with a lie, you are bitterly cursed. You, among all living things, will crawl on your belly and eat the dust of the ground all the days of your life. And there will be hostility between you and the woman and between her seed and your seed. Her child will crush your head, but you will only bruise his heel."[41]

This curse on the animal was symbolic. The actual curse was pronounced upon the angel Lucifer, who was not around but very much before the eyes of the Lord. It was the last Adam that would bring the death blow to Lucifer.

The Lord then said to him, "Your name is no longer Lucifer, but you shall be called Satan (which means *accuser*)." It was little known to Satan that God would now use him to achieve His will and purposes according to His sovereign plan.

The literal serpent animal itself was a very beautiful but crafty and cunning creature. As God pronounced the curse, suddenly the serpent lost his legs and fell to the ground in the form of what we know to this day as a snake. Just looking into the face and eyes of a snake gives a hint of what the original serpent looked like. Its countenance reflects an evil, cunning, but wise expression producing fear and intimidation. Many snakes possess poisonous venom, reminding us of the poison of sin, which was introduced into the human race by Satan. As a result of this poison, we experience pain, sorrow, sickness, and death in this world.

While this was happening, Lucifer was boasting of his success in obtaining the title deed to the earth and how he now had all authority to rule over the new creation through man. He was shouting, "I am as powerful as God himself, and I will be as the Most High God, and I will rule over all creation."

Many more of the angels believed in him and so joined him in this evil quest. However, what they did not take into account was the prophetic word from God of their oncoming defeat. Through another Adam, who would come through the seed of a woman, Satan and his seed would be destroyed.

In all, Satan managed to deceive a third of the angels in Ooranos to follow him.[42]

Then Love turned to the woman and said, "Woman, as a result of what you have done, your pain in birthing children will increase, and in sorrow you will bring them forth. And your desire will be to dominate your husband, but he will rule over you. This is the nature of sin's force."

Then Love said to Adam, "Adam, because you listened to your wife and have eaten from the tree, which I commanded you not to eat, cursed is the ground because of you. It will now be full of thorns and thistles, and only by the sweat of your brow will it produce food for you. And then in time you will return to the ground from which you came. From dust you came, and to dust you shall return." (This is when Adam, by faith, named his wife Eve.)

Chapter 10

Redemption Revealed

Love then tenderly said, "Adam, I cannot accept your fig leaf coverings. So because I love you and will always love you with an everlasting love, I have prepared a covering for you. The covering I offer you is of my own choosing. It is my way of covering your sin and nakedness before me and not your way. It must be through the shedding of innocent blood. If any man will receive my covering for their sin and shame, they too will find forgiveness and be released from the penalty of their sins.[43]

"I have shed the blood of an innocent lamb and made coverings for each of you. This lamb will symbolize the Lamb of God, who will someday come and give his life for the sins of all men. If you will have faith in my promise and accept my offering and teach your children to do the same, this sacrifice will then be the assurance of life to you and all your descendants.

"The Lamb that is to come will be wholly righteous and without sin. He will be the final sacrifice. Anyone by faith who is clothed with the coat of His righteousness and not the fig leaves of self-righteousness will be considered righteous.

"You will find the life that is eternal in my provision, and what you have lost will be restored to you through the last Adam to come. I will make an everlasting covenant

with Him, and in the volume of the Book of God, His voice will declare your innocence once again. Then man will be returned to his original origin, state, and dignity by grace through faith.[44] Hold to this promise, and you will live."

Adam said, "Lord, we will trust you, and if it pleases you, we will accept your covering and also teach our children to bring to you the blood sacrifice that you desire as a sign of our faith in your promise. For great is our sin, but you are to be praised and trusted, for your grace is out of all proportion far greater than our sin. Praise be to your name."

"Adam, you must take your wife and leave the garden. You will till the ground from which you were taken until that day that you shall return to it. But remember, I will always love you, and although it will not be the same as it was in the garden, I will still be near you. So call on me, you and your children, and I will answer. Trust in me and you will live in the promise of the life to come."

With heads bowed low, with pain in their hearts, and tears streaming from their eyes, the man and his wife walked out of the garden through the east gate. A great sense of fear was upon them, for they did not know what the future had in store for them. The joy of the paradise and the fellowship they had enjoyed with Love would never be the same for them in this world.

The east gate was the only entrance into the garden. As they passed through the gate and looked over their shoulders, they saw a sign above the gate that read, "You are entering Eden, The Garden of God, wherein lies the Tree of Life." An angel of the Lord was then stationed at the gate, and a great flaming sword that swirled in every direction was placed there to guard access to the Tree of Life.

Adam would forever long for the embrace of Love, for he knew what it was like to touch God. He also came to know the true meaning of love, but that love, the joy, the peace that he experienced in his Maker's presence, would now only be a distant memory. There would only be a remnant of that love through one of the most precious gifts that God had given him, Eve. And the scar in his side would be a constant reminder of Love's promise, that one day another Adam would come and all that was lost would once again be restored. Adam thought to himself, *To choose to truly love another is to accept the pain that it demands, the pain of dying to self in the best interest of another, regardless of feelings.*

Chapter 11

Life Outside
the Garden

Adam and Eve's first days and nights outside of the garden were full of depression and anxiety. Regret and lingering shame dominated their thoughts and conversation. It was hard for them to accept the results of their transgression. One sin had caused them the loss of eternal life in a paradise and brought them into a harsh and uncertain world.

Everything did not change immediately outside the garden. Food was plentiful, not much different from inside, so there was plenty to eat. The sun rose every morning, and the stars filled the night sky. However, they kept in mind that God had said, that the ground was now cursed, and it would only yield its fruit by the sweat of their brow. It was only a matter of time before thorns and thistles would overcome the land.

As the light of their first day outside the garden began to fade, they found a place to retire for the evening that was beyond the view of the garden gate and the flaming sword. As they were ensuring each other with an embrace, Eve said to Adam. "Husband, I am so ashamed for what I caused. Will you ever be able to forgive me?"

Adam said, "Do not blame yourself, my wife, for it was I who made the choice. You are my wife for as long as we live. I will always love you more than my own life. How could I ever do less to you than the Lord has done to me, by forgiving me?" Adam reassured her of his love for her.

The following morning, they began to feel a little more positive but noticed some little changes from what they were used to in the garden. Adam noticed that many of the animals that they befriended in the garden were now acting skittish and estranged. His friend the parrot was still the same, but the leopard was now keeping his distance and not approaching them.

Eve said to Adam, "Why isn't *Shachar* coming to us any longer? He seems to be afraid of us."

"I don't know, Eve. Something has changed in them; even our horses that we ride seem to keep their distance. It seems that our sin has affected the entire world. Let's see if we can come near the horses and ride them. We can ride toward the mountains and decide where we want to make our home here outside the garden."

The horses did let them approach, so they rode along the bank of one of the four rivers, called the Euphrates that flowed from the mountains that were northwest of the garden. The day was beautiful, full of sunshine, as usual. They rode across a large open, grassy plain toward a forest of huge trees in front of them. As they approached the edge of the forest that lined the base of the mountain range, their thoughts of the garden became less dominant. Their attention was now turned to the breathtaking beauty of the mountain forest before them and the immediate task at hand, to find a dwelling place to settle and start their life over.

They rode until they came to the edge of the forest where they could look back over the plain to the southeast and see the garden. To the northwest was a view of a rocky mountainside where a waterfall flowed from the side of a cliff and terminated into a still pool of water at its base, then into a slow moving stream that flowed past them into the river.

Adam said, "If it is pleasing to you, my love, let us settle here that you may bring forth our children in this land. I will plant a garden and raise sheep, goats, and cattle here."

"May the Lord give you the desires of your heart, my husband, and may I be a helpmate to you in this place. It seems to be a good place to raise our children. Yes, let us settle here."

So Adam and his wife settled there and named their home after the river they had followed, Euphrates of the land of Eden. The river's name meant *to break forth* and the word Eden meant *sweet and fruitful.* So they believed by faith, that this place would provide them a pleasant and fruitful homeland.

There were three other rivers that flowed through the land of Eden. There was the Gihon River, which meant *bursting forth or gushing*; the Hiddekel River, which meant *swift or darting*; and the Pishon, which meant *dispersive, or increasing.*

In the early history of man the meaning of words were very important. The spiritual significance of these names would not be realized until centuries later when God would cause rivers of living water to flow from the hearts of His children. These rivers of living water, flowing through the hearts of men from God, would produce prosperity, excess for giving, destiny, and purpose, all bringing sweet fruitfulness not only to the children themselves, but to all those around them. This would become what is referred to as the true Christian life.[45]

As time went on, life became harder and harder. Animals became more ferocious and dangerous; pesky insects increased and became a curse in themselves. Thorns and thistles dominated much of the fields as God said they would. Adam came to experience what it meant to live by the sweat of his brow.

The garden of Eden slowly disappeared as vines and weeds took the place of the lush and bountiful environment. All the trees, the plants, and even the vine fence and gate crumbled and decomposed into the ground, leaving not even a trace. Access to the Tree of Life would now only be found in the reality of the spiritual realm.

However, in spite of the curse, Adam was blessed by the Lord with much produce and many flocks of sheep, goats, and cattle. Eve also was fruitful in bringing forth many children, but for many years only daughters were born to her.[46]

The daughters learned how to live off the land, becoming tillers of the ground and shepherds of the field. Many helped their mother make clothing and do other domestic chores. The more adventurous joined their father as he began to explore, divide, and map the land around Eden into various territories, giving each of them a name. Some of the daughters began to settle and make their own homes in these lands, which was the beginning of various towns and cities.

Eve was approaching her hundredth year, and she said to Adam, "Husband, our daughters are beginning to ask if there will ever be husbands for them, that they might bear children. They are many and need husbands, but the Lord has not yet given us one male child. With so much increase, you also need strong sons that can help you in the fields."

Adam said, "I will present an offering to the Lord and there bring this matter before Him."

The Lord answered Adam and said to him. "Adam, your wife will conceive and bring forth a male child and you shall name him Cain (meaning *a fast-striking spear*). Unknown to Adam was that this son would become a violent son with a hot temper.

Nine months later Eve gave birth to Cain. She said, "I have gotten a male child from the Lord. He has removed my anguish and replaced it with joy."

Adam then brought an offering to the Lord and the Lord again spoke to him and said, "Adam, soon your wife will conceive and again bring forth a male son, and you shall call his name Abel," meaning *vain*. This son's name would signify the vanity of his life, not referring to the quality of his life, but to its short duration, for it would be cut short in an early death.

Adam and Eve treasured their boys and told them the story of the garden and the results of their transgression over and over many times. They instructed them to have faith in God and how to demonstrate that faith by bringing a sacrificial offering of an innocent lamb to the Lord. The boys were instructed to seek the presents of the Lord, for He was always near.

Cain learned from his father how to till the ground and to grow fruits and vegetables of all sorts. Abel became a shepherd, watching over the family herds of sheep, goats, and cattle. Life was a constant challenge for the family to keep the weeds and animals from destroying their crops, but life overall was good.

Chapter 12

The Anointed Seed
is Preserved

For over a hundred years, Adam and his family lived in Euphrates, in the land of Eden, as well as many of the surrounding lands that he had established.

One day the two boys, Cain and Abel, decided to bring an offering to the Lord. Abel remembered what his father Adam had taught him, that the sacrifice the Lord desired was one of faith. Cain on the other hand had his own idea of what would please God.

To be a sacrifice of faith, it had to be what the Lord established, which was a blood sacrifice of an unblemished lamb. In this way man would be making a faith statement, believing the promise of God, that in the future he was going to provide a once-and-for-all sacrifice for man's sins through the shedding of innocent blood. For by the transgression of the one man, all became guilty. The sin of the first Adam was passed on to all men, but by the righteousness and perfection of the last Adam (who was to be Jesus Christ), all would, by the gift of God, be declared innocent and guiltless in God's sight. The only requirement would be to receive the gift by grace through faith. That is, the gift that God offers man, not the gift that man would offer God.

So it came about in the course of time that Cain brought from the fruits of the land a sacrifice to the

Lord. Although he knew what his father had told him, that the Lord desired a blood sacrifice, he thought to himself, *I have a better idea. Surely, God will much more appreciate a gift from the works of my own hands rather than acquiring a lamb from my brother.*

Abel, however, by faith brought the firstborn of his sheep and their fat portions as his sacrifice. And the Lord was pleased with Abel's offering but had no regard for Cain's offering. As a result Cain became very distressed and angry, this showed on his face.[47]

God then spoke to Cain and said, "Why are you so angry, Cain? And why the long face? If you had done what is required, you would not be downcast but accepted and lifted up. The sin of your anger wants to control you, but you must control it."

Cain then said to the Lord, "What is wrong with my sacrifice? I worked long hours in the field producing the fruits that I brought to you. Is not the work of my own hands a good thing? Why is that not pleasing to you?"

"Cain, I understand and appreciate your intentions, but there is a broad road that is paved with good intensions, and that road leads to destruction. Is it too much for me to expect simple faith in the word of my promise? Did not your parents teach you this? If you will just trust me and do what I ask, whether you understand it or not, you will be accepted. You replaced faith with the self-righteous work of religion, which is not faith.

"A religious spirit will always seek to please me in ways that are not in accordance with faith. It despises my way by replacing it with manmade gifts of self-sacrifice. However, man can only please me by faith, and faith works through love and love trusts at all times. But religion works through self-righteous works and fear. It is birthed from the Tree of the Knowledge of Good and Evil. But you must train your senses to discern what is beautiful and what is worthless in my sight."

Cain was not hearing what God was saying, for his ears were deafened by his anger. His mind was an oxymoronic field of self-justification through self-pity on the one hand, and fearful and sorrowful regret on the other. Cain would remain angry and unrepentant throughout the rest of his life.

Satan, who was taking in all that was transpiring, met with his leading servants and said, "I believe that Adam's second born might be the promised seed that was foretold to come and defeat me. So we shall use the anger of his brother to take him out of the way." So when God departed, Satan entered into Cain.

Cain then said to his brother, "Come, Abel, let's go into the fields, I have something to show you there."

After traveling some distance into a field that was surrounded with tall grass, Abel said, "What is it you want to show me, brother?"

Cain said, "Over there, brother; look over there."

As Abel looked away in the direction that Cain was pointing, Cain's face turned bright red, and the veins in his neck swelled as he picked up a large stone and stuck his brother upon the head. Able fell forward onto the ground, holding his head and crying out in pain Cain jumped upon Abel's body and struck him again and again with hard blows to the head, screaming, "You think you are better than me! I will show you! God will not receive anymore sacrifices from you!"

When Cain stopped striking Abel's body, blood was everywhere. Then suddenly as if coming out of a trance, Cain dropped the stone and looked at his hands and legs that were covered with his brother's blood. As he sat there on the still body, he realized the horror of what he had just done. He jumped up and began to run aimlessly through the fields until falling into a small stream of water where he tore off his clothes and franticly tried to wash the blood from his stained body with wet sand and water. He scrubbed himself until his skin burned and then rose up and ran again, this time naked until he found a place to hide.

As he hid under some bushes in confusion and fear, he was startled by God's voice.

"Cain, where is your brother Abel?"

Cain angrily fired back, "How do I know? Am I my brother's keeper?"

"I know what you have done, Cain. For the voice of your brother's blood is crying out to me from the ground. The ground, which has received your brother's blood from the violence of your own hands, will now be cursed to you. When you till the ground, it will no longer yield its fruitful strength to you; you are to become a fugitive and a vagabond in the earth, and you will see my face no more."

Cain was without remorse and concern for the death of his brother and the grief it was going to bring to his parents. He was only concerned about himself. He said to the Lord, "This punishment is too great for me to bear! You are this day cursing the ground to me, your face shall be hidden from me, and all men will want to kill me because of what I have done. I will be a fugitive and a wanderer in the earth."

"Let it be known, Cain, that if anyone kills you, vengeance will be taken on them sevenfold."

Then Cain left the presence of the Lord and fled from the land of Eden, for he did not want to face his parents. He settled in the land of Nod, east of the land of Eden, and there he took one of his sisters as a wife, who gave birth to many sons and daughters of Cain.

After speaking to Cain, the Lord appeared to Adam and said, "Adam, I have painful news for you and your wife. Your son, Cain, has killed his brother Abel, and his body lies in the field of Cain. You are to retrieve his body and bury him there in order to redeem that field. At the grave of Abel, you shall place a marker there that reads, 'Anyone who avenges Abel's death by killing Cain will be avenged sevenfold.'

"Grieve not for Abel, for he has entered into rest, and you will one day see him again, but grieve for your son

Cain, for he feels no remorse except for himself, and he will suffer much loss in this life and the life to come."

Adam and Eve immediately dropped what they were doing and ran to the fields of Cain. Many of their daughters, seeing their distress, ran after them. They ran through the fields frantically searching until they arrived at the spot where Abel's still body lay. In horror and unbelief, they fell upon the body weeping. A storm of tears streamed from their eyes as their hearts broke in agonizing pain. Eve screamed with a loud voice. "Why has the Lord done this thing to us?" It is because of my sin that he has done this!

Many of the daughters began to wail and shout with loud cries, some of them falling upon the backs of their parents in an attempt to console them.

As they lay upon the body weeping, Love and many heavenly hosts were surrounding them. As Love saw their sorrow, his heart broke. He began to weep for them with tears of compassion.

He said, "Oh Father, what have we done, that we have made man in our image and our likeness and gave him free will? The pain of his sin is too much to bear, if only there were another way. The man even blames us for this evil."

"Son, you know that in your love for mankind, you must suffer much pain, but you must endure it for the joy set before you. We know now that natural man lives in the flesh and only knows what he sees. Eve cries out from what she sees and does not understand, but her joy will return to her in time. It is the desire of the Evil One to turn the hearts of the children against us and to blame us for all that is evil."

"Yes, Father, man will never understand our ways until he becomes one with us."

Love knew that one day he himself would have to bear the pain of man's sins, grief, and sorrows in order to free man from sin's curse. Then man and God could become one, just as the Father and the Son are one. But until that time there would be much pain and sorrow because of what man would bring upon himself.

Adam and Eve mourned for many months over the loss of Abel, but not only this, they also lost Cain as well. Although being much alive, he separated himself from his parents because of his guilt and shame. When he did see them, he ran, for he did not want to face them. Cain's bitterness grew so that his heart became increasingly hardened toward Love. Cain never brought another sacrifice to God.

In the course of time, Love came to Adam and said, "Rejoice, for your wife will again conceive and bring forth a male son who will return to her the joy that was taken from her. This son will father the royal line of the Prince who is to come, the last Adam."

And it came to pass in the hundred and thirtieth-fifth year of Adam's life that Eve gave birth to another son whom they named Seth. Eve, with great joy, said, "Look! The Lord has given me another son in the place of Abel, who Cain killed. Praise be to the name of the Lord!"

Adam lived eight hundred years after the birth of Seth and fathered many more sons and daughters.

It was after the birth of Seth that many men began to call upon the name of the Lord.

End Notes

Preface: Notes 1 - 5

1 John 3:17 tells us that it was never God's intention to condemn man but to save him: For God sent not his Son into the world to condemn the world; but that the world through him might be saved.

   John 3:18: He that believeth on him is not condemned; but he that believeth not is condemned already, because he hath not believed in the name of the only begotten Son of God.

2 1Jn 4:8 He that loveth not knoweth not God; for God is love.

   1Jn 4:16 And we have known and believed the love that God hath to us. God is love; and he that dwelleth in love dwelleth in God, and God in him.

3 In Ephesians 1:4 we read: According as he hath chosen us in him before the foundation of the world, that we *should be* holy and without blame before him in love:

   The phrase *should be holy* is misleading. This is an improper translation. The meaning of the Greek word means *to exist as*. We do not strive to become holy; we exist as holy in the new creation man. We bring forth holy living from the new creation; the flesh profits nothing. This is so essential to walking in the spirit so that we will not fulfill the lusts of the flesh. Holiness in not doing, it's being.

4   Jeremiah 29:11: "For I know the plans that I have for you, declares the LORD, plans for welfare and not for calamity to give you a future and a hope." (NASB)

5   Genesis 5:7 demonstrates that out of love, man (male and female) create another man in their image. This reflects how love works in the Trinity.

Chapter 1: Notes 6 - 14

6   This was not the first morning in creation, it was the man's first morning in the garden.

7   Ooranos is the English pronunciation of the Greek word for heaven, ouranos. It is the NT word for the abode of God. It is not a place beyond the universe but it refers to another dimension which contains the universe we see.

8   The root for original Hebrew word *ground* in Genesis 2:7: Then the LORD God formed man of dust from the *ground*... and the word *blood* in Leviticus 17:11 is the same word: For the life of the flesh is in the blood, and I have given it to you on the altar to make atonement for your souls; for it is the *blood* by reason of the life that makes atonement. The dust of the earth was used by God to make blood, thus, physical life possible. We can not have physical life without it. The blood of Jesus gives us eternal life. Without it, we have no hope of eternal life. This is why God established the blood sacrifices of animals: To show man what is necessary to obtain life eternal.

9 When God made man, He looked at Himself then said, "Let Us make a man in our image." This makes us unique from animals and angels. We are beings made in the image and likeness of God, all others are creatures.

10 John 17:5: And now, O Father, glorify thou me with thine own self with the glory which I had with thee before the world was.

John 17:24: Father, I will that they also, whom thou hast given me, be with me where I am; that they may behold my glory, which thou hast given me: for thou lovedst me before the foundation of the world.
In the Septuagint, *other* is *heteros* of a different kind. We are the God kind in likeness and image. He does not give His glory to another of a different kind but He does to us.
John 17:22: praise to graven images (carved image or quarry. Exodus 20:25, 1Kings 6:7, Isaiah 51:1: but He does to us.
Ephesians 1:12, Ephesians 1:6: For we are made in His image.
Acts 17:29

11 Revelation 4:11: Thou art worthy, O Lord, to receive glory and honour and power: for thou hast created all things, and for thy pleasure they are and were created.

12 The term *The Word* comes from the original Greek word *o logos*, which is used in John 1:1: In the beginning was the Word… The original word *logos* means, *The Divine Expression*. It does not refer to a written word, but one that is spoken or expressed. Primarily it is the expression of God's life through Christ. This is why Jesus said, "If you have seen me, you

have seen the Father." He expressed the life of God to us. In contrast, the Greek word *rhema* is the voice of God. *Logos* is the expression of mental thought and logic through *rhema* or actions, not just oratory or the voicing of words. *Logos* has everything to do with the meaning of what is spoken or expressed. Again, in contrast, the word *rhema* refers to the voice only, not the meaning of what is said.

13 2Peter 1:3: According as his divine power hath given unto us all things that *pertain* unto life and godliness, through the knowledge of him that hath called us to glory and virtue.

14 The closer we draw to Christ, the more light we see and the less darkness we experience. The things in this world grow dim when we are consumed with His marvelous light. I believe this is what we experience when we are baptized in the Holy Spirit. The word *baptized* in the original Greek means *to immerse*. The baptism of the Holy Spirit means to be immersed into the presence of God, and God is light.

15 Some may ask, "Does God really give hugs?" The idea that God literally embraced Adam is of course, speculative. However, the reason I believe He did is because it is a natural action for any parent to embrace a newborn child. I reasoned, "Why would it be any different with God?" In the New Testament however, we have scriptural support for the spiritual embrace of God. In the following verses, Acts 20:37, Acts 10:44, and Acts 20:10, the Greek word for *embrace* is used of an act of the Holy Spirit. It is translated *fell upon*, but in our language we would say, "bear hug or embrace." The same word is used in Luke 15:20: And he arose, and came

to his father. But when he was yet a great way off, his father saw him, and had compassion, and ran, and fell on his neck, and kissed him.

The words *fell upon* should be translated embraced.

Chapter 2: Notes 15 - 18

16 Song of Solomon 5:1: I am come into my garden, my sister, *my* spouse: I have gathered my myrrh with my spice; I have eaten my honeycomb with my honey; I have drunk my wine with my milk: eat, O friends; drink, yea, drink abundantly, O beloved.

Song of Solomon 6:2: My beloved is gone down into his garden, to the beds of spices, to feed in the gardens, and to gather lilies.

17 There are only two proposed theories of how life began. If one is disproved, then it proves the other to be true. The mathematical science of probabilities proves that the theory of evolution is impossible, that leaves only the alternative to be the true reality, creation by divine intelligence.

The limit of something to be possible ends at the probability factor of, one in ten to the fiftieth power. That is the point of impossible. Presently, evolutionists tell us that the probability of life beginning from one cell is; one in ten to the one thousand power. To put this in perspective, consider this example. It would be like an ameba, taking every atom in the universe, one at a time, and crossing the entire universe, moving at one inch every billion years. This is the same probability that evelotion is true.

18 The 3 rests of God: The Creation of the Father, The Redemptive rest of Christ, and the Holy Spirit's resting… the Thought, Word, and Deed are illustrated in these three rests.

19 Here is the basic meanings of some bible numbers:

1 Oneness, One God, one family, one Relationship

2 Witness, Two Establishes the event as Fact

3 Fellowship, Triune (Trinity) Nature of God

4 Earth, the Physical realm, Earth and the things of it. There are four corners to the earth.

5 Grace, Favor of God, that is: The divine influence upon the heart and it's reflection in the life.

6 Number of Man. Natural man, man without God is Incomplete.

7 Complete Perfection. Not necessarily and event. For example; The seven spirits of God referred to in the book of Revelation; refer to the complete and perfect Holy Spirit of God. The number 10 is different. Means completeness also, but refers to a completeness in general.

8 Newness, New Beginnings, New Day, New Outlook, Jesus' Number. The name Jesus in the Greek is equal to 888.

9 Ordained, Fullness of God's Ordained Plan (3) x (3) = 9

10 A completeness. Might be an event or law, or people. For example; 4x10=40. 4 is the number of earth, 10 shows that

the flood was a earthly event that was complete. The ten commandments; summaries God's complete law. Ten tribes of Israel; Complete nation.

12 Number of the church, the body or bride of Christ. Example; 144,000 in the book or Revelation is the complete church. 12X12X10X10X10=144,000.

13 Evil, man attempting to be equal with God, Satan's number

40 A complete earth event. For example; the flood.

70 Seven times ten. Perfect and complete event

1000 A number that means; unmeasurable or an uncertain time period

Chapter 3: Notes 19 – 22

20 **Covenants** are an important feature of the Bible's teaching. Seven specific covenants are revealed in Scripture. These seven covenants fall into three categories—conditional, unconditional, and general. Conditional covenants are based on certain obligations and prerequisites; if the requirements are not fulfilled, the covenant is broken. Unconditional covenants are made with no strings attached and will be kept regardless of one party's fidelity or infidelity. General covenants are not specific to one people group and can involve a wide range of people.

The conditional covenant mentioned in Scripture is the Mosaic Covenant; the blessings it extends are contingent upon Israel's adherence to the Law. The unconditional covenants mentioned in the Bible are the Abrahamic, Palestinian, and Davidic Covenants; God promises to fulfill these regardless of other factors. The general covenants mentioned are the Adamic, Noahic, and New Covenants, which are global in scope. Each of these covenants is listed below in biblical order with a brief description:

1. **Adamic Covenant.** Found in Genesis 1:26-30 and 2:16-17, this covenant is general in nature. It included the command not to eat from the tree of the knowledge of good and evil, pronounced a curse for sin, and spoke of a future provision for man's redemption (Genesis 3:15).

2. **Noahic Covenant.** This general covenant was made between God and Noah following the departure of Noah, his family, and the animals from the ark. Found in Genesis 9:11, "I establish my covenant with you, that never again shall all flesh be cut off by the waters of the flood, and never again shall there be a flood to destroy the earth." This covenant included a sign of God's faithfulness to keep it—the rainbow.

3. **Abrahamic Covenant.** This unconditional covenant, first made to Abraham in Genesis 12:1-3, promised God's blessing upon Abraham, to make his name great and to make his progeny into a great nation. The covenant also promised blessing to those who blessed Abraham and cursing to those who cursed him. Further, God vowed to bless the entire world through Abraham's seed. Circumcision was the sign that Abraham believed the covenant (Romans 4:11). The fulfillment of this covenant is seen in the history of Abraham's descendants and

in the creation of the nation of Israel. The worldwide blessing came through Jesus Christ, who was of Abraham's family line.

4. **Palestinian Covenant.** This unconditional covenant, found in Deuteronomy 30:1-10, noted God's promise to scatter Israel if they disobeyed God, then to restore them at a later time to their land. This covenant has been fulfilled, with the Babylonian Captivity and subsequent rebuilding of Jerusalem under Cyrus the Great. With the destruction of Jerusalem in A.D. 70 God then divorced himself from the natural Israel. (Jer 3:8)

5. **Mosaic Covenant.** This conditional covenant, found in Deuteronomy 11 and elsewhere, promised the Israelites a blessing for obedience and a curse for disobedience. Much of the Old Testament chronicles the fulfillment of this cycle of judgment for sin and later blessing when God's people repented and returned to God.

6. **Davidic Covenant.** This unconditional covenant, found in 2 Samuel 7:8-16, promised to bless David's family line and assured an everlasting kingdom. Jesus is from the family line of David (Luke 1:32-33) and, as the Son of David (Mark 10:47), is the fulfillment of this covenant.

7. **New Covenant.** This covenant, found in Jeremiah 31:31-34, promised that God would forgive sin and have a close, unbroken relationship with His people. The promise was made both to Jew and Gentile. The promise of eternal life extends to everyone who comes to Jesus Christ in faith. The blood covenant that gives us this promise was made between God the Father and

Jesus. Man's only part to play, is by faith, to believe and receive.

While not all Bible scholars agree on every detail regarding these biblical covenants, it is clear that God has made certain promises. Some of His promises are to all people, and some are limited to Israel. All of God's promises are based on who He is and His plan for the world. Under the New Covenant, which Jesus sealed with His own blood, everyone is offered salvation by grace through faith. "And it shall come to pass that everyone who calls upon the name of the Lord shall be saved" (Acts 2:21).

Used with permission from: Gotquestions.org.

21 1John 4:16: And we have known and believed the love that God hath to us. God is love; and he that dwelleth in love dwelleth in God, and God in him.

22 John 1:3: All things were made by him; and without him was not any thing made that was made.

23 This was a prophetic word given by Love. The she referred to the Church; the Bride of Christ, that would be brought forth from Jesus, into his eternal rest. This is why I have Eve being created on the seventh day. Although it is true that God rested on the seventh day from all His works, I thought it could be possible that Eve, as a type of the Church, would be created or brought forth in God's rest, just as Christians today are everyday being brought into His eternal rest.

24 Genesis 1:27: So God created man in his *own* image, in the image of God created he him; male and female created he them.

25 1Corinthians 11:7: For a man indeed ought not to cover *his* head, forasmuch as he is the image and glory of God: but the woman is the glory of the man.

26 God here is the one who brings the bride to the groom. In both Jewish and Christian tradition, the father of the bride presents, or gives, the bride to the groom. Showing that Eve was a gift from Father God to Adam.

27 Simply stated, the idea of *creation with appearance of age* means that when God created, those things that He created might superficially have looked as if they had a history. When Adam was created, he no doubt looked like a mature adult, fully able to walk, talk, care for the garden, etc. When God created fruit trees, they were already bearing fruit. In each case, what He created was functionally complete right from the start, able to fulfill the purpose for which it was created. Stars, created on Day Four, had to be seen to perform their purpose of usefulness in telling time; therefore, their light had to be visible on earth right from the start. God's evaluation that the completed creation was *very good* necessitated that it be functionally complete, operating in harmony, with each part fulfilling the purpose for which it was created.

28 Ezekiel 28:15: Thou *wast* perfect in thy ways from the day that thou wast created, till iniquity was found in thee.

29 The question, "Why was Satan in the garden?" is a hard one. We are not told why or how, but I speculated that God sent him. Drawing the conclusion that Lucifer and Satan are in fact the same angel is based on the following scriptures.

Isaiah14:12-15. The context of this passage is a referral to the king of Babylon as presented in his pride, splendor, and fall. However, it is to the power behind the evil Babylonian king that this is actually addressed. No mortal king would claim that his throne was above that of God or that he was like the Most High. The power behind the evil Babylonian king is Lucifer, Son of the Morning.

Ezekiel 28:11-19. As in the Isaiah passage, this passage similarly seems to be addressed to the *king of Tyre*. In reality, it goes beyond the king to the one who is behind the evil king of Tyre. This passage also has near and far prophecy about Lucifer/Satan because, although his final end is already sure, it has not happened yet and it occurs after the final judgment. Compare Revelation 20:7-10. Notice the statement that is given in the passage in Ezekiel, *the anointed cherub*. These statements could never apply to a human king but, they do apply to Lucifer/Satan, who is behind the human king.

There are many more passages that you can consider, but it is not the purpose of this book to do a complete study on the subject.

30 Man was given through the Adamic covenant rule an authority over the earth. I do not believe that Satan has or ever had any real, individual authority over the earth because man had the authority. So, the only way that Satan could rule was in and through the man. This he does both through influence and possession.

Chapter 6: Notes 30 - 32

31 In Genesis 1:1 and over 2,000 other times in the Old Testament appears the Hebrew word for God, *Elohim*. *Elohim* is the plural from of the word *El*. Ancient Hebrews believed and taught that God was a triune God, that is, He is one God in essence, who manifests himself as three distinct persons.

32 The reason I believe that Adam and Eve had sexual relations before the fall is because man was created for intimacy. God created the act to reflect the highest form of intimacy that man could experience, and it was pure. It was to reflect in the physical what the spiritual was to be between man and God.

If Adam and Eve did not have sexual relations until after the fall, sex would have then become only a carnal act of the fallen man. However, having relations before the fall established the sex act as a pure and divine gift; as pure and good as all that God created. So sex in the garden between Adam and his wife demonstrates the purity of sexual relations. However, I do not believe that Eve conceived until after the fall for obvious reasons. Mainly, that there would have been a sinless child birthed by sinful parents.

33 This temptation that was brought to Eve by the tempter was the same temptation that was brought to Jesus in the wilderness.

It is the same temptation that is brought to us by Satan. It's always one or more of the same three. It is written that Jesus was tempted in every area that we are tempted. This temptation in the wilderness was what was referred to when it says that he was tempted in every area that we are tempted. He was tempted by: the lust of the eyes, the lust of the flesh, and the pride of life, just as Eve was. But, Jesus, the last Adam, would not fail the test as did the first Adam. Compare the temptation that came to Eve with the following temptation of Jesus.

Matthew 4:3: And when the tempter came to him, he said, If thou be the Son of God, command that these stones be made bread.-*Temptation of the flesh.*

Matthew 4:4: But he answered and said, It is written, Man shall not live by bread alone, but by every word that proceedeth out of the mouth of God.

Matthew 4:5: Then the devil taketh him up into the holy city, and setteth him on a pinnacle of the temple,

Matthew 4:6: And saith unto him, If thou be the Son of God, cast thyself down: for it is written, He shall give his angels charge concerning thee: and in *their* hands they shall bear thee up, lest at any time thou dash thy foot against a stone.-*Temptation of the pride of life.*

Matthew 4:7: Jesus said unto him, It is written again, Thou shalt not tempt the Lord thy God.

Matthew 4:8: Again, the devil taketh him up into an exceeding high mountain, and sheweth him all the kingdoms of the world, and the glory of them;-*Temptation of the lust of the eyes.*

Matthew 4:9: And saith unto him, all these things will I give thee, if thou wilt fall down and worship me.

Matthew 4:10: Then saith Jesus unto him, Get thee hence, Satan: for it is written, Thou shalt worship the Lord thy God, and him only shalt thou serve.

Matthew 4:11: Then the devil leaveth him.

There are several great lesson for us to learn here. First, when we are tempted to sin, we can know it is always in one of these three areas; the same three that Christ himself was tempted. Hebrews 4:15: For we have not an high priest which cannot be touched with the feeling of our infirmities; but was in all points tempted like as we are, yet without sin.

The second thing is that we can do exactly what Jesus did, and the devil will flee. Notice in every temptation, Jesus just submitted himself to God by submitting to the truth of God's word, and after three times the devil fled. James 4:7: Submit yourselves therefore to God. Resist the devil, and he will flee from you. It worked for him, it will work for us.

34 We know from the book of Job that Satan had access to God before he was cast out of heaven. He accused us before God continually until Christ finished his work on the cross, and then Satan was cast out. He can no longer accuse man before God.

35 The power of sin is the law. (1Corinthians 15:56 NAB)

Chapter 8: Notes 35 – 39

36 The fig tree in later centuries would come to symbolize the nation of Israel. The leaves of a fig tree, covering the tree itself, symbolized the Jewish religion under the Law of Moses, which we more commonly refer to as The Ten Commandments and all the other laws in the Torah. Just as Adam and Eve's fig leaves would fail to be an acceptable covering for their sin and shame before God, so would Israel's attempt to cover their sin with the inadequacy of law based religion for righteousness. The fig leaf aprons were symbolic of man's self-righteous attempt to cover his sin and shame before God. The law, however, was never given with the intent of producing righteousness, but just the opposite. It would become the power of sin to show man that even in his best efforts he would still fall short of his original glory for which he was created, which glory was only found in his Creator.

The aprons that Adam and Eve made were made to cover the reproductive organs. The reason for this is because the sexual act in marriage between a man and a woman was the highest natural expression of intimacy that they would experience. This act, like no other, symbolizes the greatest spiritual intimacy that can exist between man and God. When they sinned, this understanding was lost, and God's nature of love became distorted and twisted in the minds of natural men. Through the fall, natural man would lose the true meaning of love turning love into lust.

37 The word *myrtle*, as used in Scripture, is Strong's 1918 *hadac*. When we look at these Hebrew letters, we come to the meaning of this tree;

Hey: Symbolic meaning; the, to reveal. Literal meaning; Behold.

Dalet: Symbolic meaning; pathway to enter. Literal meaning; Door.

Shamech: Symbolic meaning; to support, twist slowly, turn. Literal meaning; Prop.

So what does this tell us of the myrtle? The first two letters *Hey* and *Dalet* show us a picture of *Behold the Door*, or *To reveal the pathway to enter*. The final letter, *Shamech*, is the prop or support and thus prevents the closing. Therefore, in one sentence the myrtle pictures *Behold the open Door*. Thus, the myrtle reveals to us the open pathway to enter.

In looking at the Scriptural meaning of the myrtle, we read in *The Illustrated Bible Dictionary* the following; "The myrtle tree had a religious significance for the Hebrews (Zech. 1:8-11) and was a symbol of peace and joy…" It is as we *enter in* that we will find *peace and joy*! It speaks of the joy of salvation to us in the new covenant, where are remembered no more by God.

38 John10:9: I am the door: by me if any man enter in, he shall be saved, and shall go in and out, and find pasture.

39 Adam and Eve both did the first requirement of salvation, to confess their sin to God. Both Adam and Eve were honest in admitting their sin.

If we say that we have no sin, we deceive ourselves, and the truth is not in us. If we confess our sins, he is faithful and just to forgive us *our* sins, and to cleanse us from all unrighteousness. (1John 1:8-9)

40 1Timothy 2:14: And *it was* not Adam *who* was deceived, but the woman being deceived, fell into transgression.

However; Romans 5:19 says: For as by one man's disobedience many were made sinners, so by the obedience of one shall many be made righteous forever.

Eve was deceived, but it was Adam's sin that made all men guilty.

Also consider Romans 5:17: For if by one man's offence death reigned by one; much more they which receive abundance of grace and of the gift of righteousness shall reign in life by one, Jesus Christ.

Chapter 9: Notes 40 - 41

41 Revelation 12:4-5: And his tail drew the third part of the stars of heaven, and did cast them to the earth: and the dragon stood before the woman which was ready to be delivered, for to devour her child as soon as it was born. And she brought forth a man child, who was to rule all nations with a rod of iron: and her child was caught up unto God, and *to* his throne.

42 Revelation 12:4: And his tail drew the third part of the stars of heaven, and did cast them to the earth: and the dragon stood before the woman which was ready to be delivered, for to devour her child as soon as it was born."

Read Revelation chapter 12 in its entirety for the whole picture.

Chapter 10: Notes 42 - 43

43 The animal sacrificed here must have been a lamb, for the sacrifice of the lamb throughout the Bible pointed to The Lamb of God, Jesus.

44 Ephesians 1:4: So by reason of this, He chose us in Him even before the foundations of the world were layed down, to exist as holy and without blame, innocent in His sight through His great love." (MIT Mirror Identity Translation)

The King James says: That we should be holy and blameless before Him in love.

However, the word *should* is misleading. The original Greek is literally *to exist*. We exist as holy; we do not attempt to be holy by self efforts. Rather, we must identify with the new man, who is made in the likeness of God, who is already complete and perfected in holiness. It is in this new man that we must walk out our life while in this flesh. If we rest in Him, walking in the Spirit, we will not fulfill the lusts of the flesh. "What a man thinks in his heart, so is he."

Chapter 11: Notes 44 - 45

45 1John 7:38 He that believeth on me, as the scripture hath said, out of his belly shall flow rivers of living water.

Rev 22:1 And he shewed me a pure river of water of life, clear as crystal, proceeding out of the throne of God and of the Lamb.

Rev 22:2 In the midst of the street of it, and on either side of the river, *was there* the tree of life, which bare twelve *manner of* fruits, *and* yielded her fruit every month: and the leaves of the tree *were* for the healing of the nations.
The passage from Revelation 22, is speaking of the living waters that proceed out of the heart of believers. We have abiding within us the the fruits of the Spirit of God for the healing of the nations. Notice that we now partake of the tree of life, who is Christ in us, the hope of glory.

46 When we ask the question, "Where did Cain get his wife?" my answer is that Eve had many daughters before she had Cain. The daughters may have established villages, or at least homes of their own, outside of Eden. Later Cain would run to one of these places for refuge and their take one of his sisters as a wife.

Chapter 12: Note 46

47 Hebrews 11:4: By faith Abel offered unto God a more excellent sacrifice than Cain, by which he obtained witness that he was righteous, God testifying of his gifts: and by it he being dead yet speaketh.